Anonymous

Report of Select Committee on Quarantine

Anatiposi

Anonymous

Report of Select Committee on Quarantine

Reprint of the original.

1st Edition 2023 | ISBN: 978-3-38230-078-4

Anatiposi Verlag is an imprint of Outlook Verlagsgesellschaft mbH.

Verlag (Publisher): Outlook Verlag GmbH, Zeilweg 44, 60439 Frankfurt, Deutschland
Vertretungsberechtigt (Authorized to represent): E. Roepke, Zeilweg 44, 60439 Frankfurt, Deutschland
Druck (Print): Books on Demand GmbH, In de Tarpen 42, 22848 Norderstedt, Deutschland

.

Chamber of Commerce.

REPORT

OF

SELECT COMMITTEE ON QUARANTINE.

ADOPTED JULY 7, 1859.

NEW YORK:

D. VAN NOSTRAND.

1859.

MR. ROYAL PHELPS, *First Vice-President, in the Chair:*

Mr. TILESTON, from the Select Committee on Quarantine, presented and read the Report of that Committee.

Ordered, That the Report be accepted and made the special order for the next Regular Meeting.

(Extract from the Minutes.)

J. SMITH HOMANS,
Secretary.

REGULAR MEETING OF THE CHAMBER,

NEW YORK, July 7, 1859.

THE PRESIDENT *in the Chair:*

The Report of the Select Committee on Quarantine, submitted by Mr. TILESTON at the last Special Meeting, was considered.

On motion of Mr. MORGAN, the Report and Resolutions were adopted unanimously, and ordered to be printed in pamphlet form.

(Extract from the Minutes.)

J. SMITH HOMANS,
Secretary.

REPORT

OF

Select Committee on Quarantine,

JUNE 29.

THE SELECT COMMITTEE appointed under the following Resolution of the Chamber, adopted at its regular meeting in May last, on motion of P. M. WETMORE, to wit,

Resolved, That the record of the proceedings of the National Quarantine and Sanitary Convention, in their session recently held in this city, on the question of the contagious nature of yellow fever, be referred to a Select Committee, with instructions to consider and report upon the general subject of the Quarantine Laws of this State, and upon the legislation required to give practical effect to the declared sentiments of the said Convention ;

And to whom was also referred the following Resolution, submitted to the Chamber for consideration at its regular meeting in June, by Mr. ROYAL PHELPS, to wit,

Resolved, That while we admit the general reasonableness of the charges for lighterage from Quarantine, as furnished by the Select Committee to the Mayor, as a general guide, it is the opinion of this Chamber that the only course which will do full justice to the merchants of New York, in the matter of lighterage, will be to throw the business open to competition from all responsible parties, subject to such rules and regulations as the Health Officer may prescribe ;

Respectfully submit the following—

REPORT.

The subject referred for the consideration of the Committee, may be treated under three different heads:

First.—The general subject of the Quarantine laws as administered by the State authorities.

Second.—The practical effect of the doctrine in regard to the non-contagiousness of yellow fever, avowed by the National Convention, in reference to future legislation on this subject.

Third.—The duty of the Chamber to insist on free competition in the business of Lighterage and other services connected therewith.

These questions have occupied the deliberate attention of the Committee, who have held several meetings for their investigation and taken testimony from intelligent and competent persons, with the view to arrive at such conclusions as may justify the future action of the Chamber.

In entering upon the discussion of these several topics, the Committee must remind the Chamber, that it has already expressed its disapprobation of the manner in which the health-laws of the port of New York have been administered, as imposing onerous and unnecessary burdens upon Commerce, and throwing needless restraints upon the personal rights and liberties of the citizen. These views of the Chamber have received additional strength and confirmation from the examination made by the Committee.

In discussing, under the first head, the general subject of the Quarantine laws, it may not be out of place to consider briefly the origin and intention of these legal restraints upon commerce, in order to judge how far it may be prudent and proper to urge their repeal or modification.

Under our own government these restrictions have existed almost from its first organization; and they prevailed, also, in some form or other under the Colonial authorities, anterior to the Revolution.

England was late in adopting the theory, which originated in Continental Europe, that external sanitary regulations could prevent the introduction and prevalence of infectious diseases.

The plague, the dreaded pestilence of ancient times, originated in Asia, and was thence introduced into Europe by way of the Mediterranean; and upon the coasts of Italy the first European lazarettos were established. The principle thus adopted, of preserving health by preventing the importation of disease, lies at the foundation of the system still maintained under our laws, and which has at last been the occasion of so many abuses that public sentiment is aroused to the necessity of demanding relief.

Rightly to understand the bearing of this question, we must view it in many of its aspects. The idea of the absolute necessity of these restrictions, as the only safeguard from pestilence, has prevailed so long and so generally, both in and out of the medical profession, that it must not lightly be dismissed, nor without the mature deliberation which its importance demands and justifies.

It is fortunate for the interests of the commercial community, that this subject has awakened public attention in other quarters than among merchants. Men of science, from the purest and most disinterested motives, have entered into the investigation with a zeal and intelligence that deserve the acknowledgments of those most deeply interested in the result. For three successive years, National Conventions have been held for the express purpose of acquiring information, eliciting facts, and establishing theories, in regard to this matter. In the cities of Philadelphia, Baltimore, and New York, these assemblages have met and given their earnest attention to the scientific elucidation of the vital question of contagion; and the final action of the recent session in this city, has brought the subject prominently before the commercial world, and has led to the institution of these proceedings.

The definition of Quarantine, as given by McCullough, who has long been regarded as authority on commercial subjects is "a regulation by which all communication with individuals, ships, or goods, arriving from *places infected with the plague or other contagious disorders*, or supposed to be peculiarly liable to such infection, is interdicted for a certain definite period."

Upon this theory has the legislation of our own State been founded, and the laws have been administered upon the unsound hypothesis that the febrile diseases to be apprehended from the commerce of the tropics were contagious. The whole action of the authorities who administered these laws, has been directed to the one object of sustaining this now exploded theory; and the consequence has been that vessels, cargoes, crews, and passengers, have been confined within the narrow compass of a quarantine station, at an enormous sacrifice of means, time, health, and life, without producing any known beneficial effect save in securing inordinate profits to officers, agents, and employes engaged in sustaining so unwise and iniquitous a system.

In other cities on the Atlantic coast, no such burdensome restrictions are placed upon the energies of commerce, as exist at this port. The evil effects of this inequality are felt in the steadily increasing diversion of trade, from this to other cities where the laws of health and the duties of precaution are better understood than with us.

In the Annual Report of the Chamber now in process of publication, the questions which come under this branch of the subject referred to the Committee, are discussed at length ; and it is, therefore, scarcely necessary to enlarge upon them at this time. The following extract from that Report, will show clearly the views entertained by the Chamber in regard to the oppressive results of the system and the practice under it :

" The principal causes of complaint and dissatisfaction in regard to existing quarantine restrictions, may be enumerated as follows:

" First.—The detention and temporary control of vessels of almost every class, whether infected or not, at the discretion of public officers and private persons, whose individual interests may be directly promoted by the delay of vessels at the quarantine station.

" Second.—The protracted detention of healthy passengers and crews, *under* '*observation*' in Quarantine, at the expense of the owners or consignees of the vessels; and the heavy taxes imposed on them for the slightest accommodations rendered necessary by their condition.

" Third.—The practice of transhipment, or lighterage of cargoes at the Quarantine anchorage, and the exorbitant charges to which merchants have hitherto been subjected therefor, solely for the promotion of private interests and objects.

" Fourth.—The risks, delay, and actual losses incident to the detention of cargoes, and the needlessly protracted anchorage of vessels at the Quarantine.

" Fifth.—The too expansive construction frequently given to existing regulations, in regard to articles of commerce which are arbitrarily deemed capable of conveying infection from one port to another."

These are among the conclusions adopted in the Annual Report; and this Committee do not hesitate to unite in the sentiment of that Report, that the abuses alluded to imperatively call for immediate reform, and that the whole system under which they prevail " requires an intelligent and judicious revision."

The Committee come now to the consideration of the second division of the subject referred for their examination. This branch of the question involves the one great principle on which the action of the Chamber is invoked; and it cannot be rightly considered without a careful and serious investigation.

If the Chamber shall come to the conclusion, adopted with singular unanimity by the National Quarantine Convention, namely: "That in the absence of any evidence establishing the conclusion that yellow fever has ever been conveyed by one person to another, it is the opinion of this Convention that personal Quarantine cases of yellow fever may be safely abolished, provided that *fomites* of every kind be rigidly restricted."—Then, clearly, so far as the judgment and action of the Chamber are concerned, its influence must stand pledged to the abrogation of restrictions upon personal liberty under the plea of precautionary restraint against the conveyance of contagion from one person to another; subject, however, in its fullest extent, to the qualification in regard to *fomites*.

Feeling the responsibility that had been devolved upon them by the Chamber, the Committee have assiduously devoted their time and attention to the investigation confided to them. It is only by this slow and painful process that truth can be arrived at and important principles established.

This subject has occupied the attention of men of science, learning, and humanity, for centuries. Merchants, though suffering most from its operation, have generally refrained from interfering in its management; and it will be a remarkable incident in its history, if after four hundred years of controversy, a question belonging as appropriately to commerce as to medical science, should be finally adjusted by a unity of sentiment and action between two professions usually so widely distinct in their interests and pursuits, as those now engaged in this investigation.

The Committee find that Quarantine originated in the medical dogma that forty days were required to test the existence of contagious infection; and accordingly, that was the period to which the restriction was limited by the wise men of Venice. It was believed by them that the forty days bounded the crisis in infectious diseases. This theory of a crisis in particular diseases remains with medical men to the present day; but its application is greatly restricted, and is as various as are many other medical theories,—ranging from forty days to seven in different shades of disease.

It is very evident that Quarantines were originally the result of fear and ignorance. Both Heathen and Christian nations, in the first centuries of the plague, believed it to be a divine punishment or predestined event, which it was impossible to avoid. The former, stoically and obstinately submitted to their fate; the latter relied for their preservation on fasting and prayer. This state of things continued down to the fourteenth century, when it was at length deemed by the Italians possible to guard against infection; and the restrictions then adopted, exclusively against contagion from the plague, have since prevailed under the governments of most commercial and civilized nations, as a general precaution against all imported diseases, down to the present day. Restrictions, therefore, commenced in the excitement of fear, have been continued in ignorance of the exact philosophy of the diseases against which they were originally established.

The Turks, the early enemies of Christendom, introduced the plague into the Levant, where even now it is occasionally seen; and its introduction was attributed to their filthy personal habits, and their ill-ventilated dwellings. It was believed to be capable of propagation under similar conditions and circumstances; though then, as now, it was difficult to determine the relative degree of infection produced by local causes arising from a pestiferous atmosphere, or from the effects of personal uncleanliness and indulgence in vicious habits. It was also found, in that day, that persons in comfortable circumstances, clean and orderly in their habits, with the enjoyment of wholesome food, good air, and pure water, generally escaped the pestilence. The object of the Quarantine was mainly, therefore, to produce the desired result by a rigid enforcement of sanitary rules on all those who came within the reach of public control.

It is a fact to be noticed, that the first who proposed and instituted these sanitary restrictions, were not the medical men of the times, as we might naturally suppose, but the police and municipal officers of the Italian cities; the establishments in Lombardy and Venice being the first of the kind of which we have any knowledge.

It is well known that persons infected with the plague were, as a general rule, removed from crowded dwellings and carried into the open air. Purification of the clothes and articles used by infected persons, was early introduced into the system of treatment; but this rule was for a time relaxed, and afterwards re-asserted and rigidly adhered to.

If it were consistent with the objects of this report, many interesting details might be given of the progress of the restrictive system, and of the laws passed by different countries to enforce it; the punishment imposed for the infraction frequently being severe, even to the infliction of death upon the violators of Quarantine regulations.

Strange as it may appear it is nevertheless true, that the laws of our own State, and the regulations under which commerce is now so seriously hampered, are founded upon precisely the same theories as those which prevailed in the unenlightened times when medical science, if it had existence at all, was in its infancy. Plague has never visited the Western continent. We import no contagious diseases save small-pox, the measles, and possibly typhus fever; and yet, for the reason that the Venetians dreaded the plague a half-dozen centuries ago, we lock up our ports against commerce under the futile apprehension that yellow fever is a contagious disease.

Every merchant interested in this subject should examine it for himself; it is too extensive to be discussed in a hastily written report of this character. A carefully arranged synopsis of the statutes of our State applying to this case, together with many interesting suggestions in regard to the general subject, was prepared some two years since, and published in one of the daily journals, by a learned, intelligent, and public-spirited citizen of New York, Mr. De Witt Bloodgood; to which reference should be made by those who desire to investigate the subject in its legal and literary aspects.

Two high foreign authorities may be referred to in reference to the theory of infectious diseases and the advantages of Quarantine regulations. Dr. McLean, of Great Britain, and the celebrated Du Pyron, Secretary of the Board of Health of France, have largely and ably discussed these topics; and it may safely be inferred from their writings that the spread of pestilential diseases is materially affected by the circumstances which attend the communication between the sick and the well; a fact which, properly understood, may explain the essential differences existing between the contagionists and non-contagionists.

Healthy persons, of good habits, in pure air, and in good condition physiologically, undoubtedly are safe from infection by contact with a diseased person, or even with his well-worn clothes; while under different circumstances, and in an infected state of the atmosphere, danger might ensue to those not properly guarded.

It is now pretty well settled that many articles of domestic use or in commerce, are not susceptible of conveying contagion, while there are others which are not innoxious, and are consequently made the special subjects of depuration; and yet it is asserted by Du Pyron that this process of purification has never been known to affect the persons engaged in the work, and that the poison has never been transmitted through goods not brought into contact with diseased persons. Although letters are elaborately fumigated in the Mediterranean ports, and restrictive rules against free correspondence insisted on with great pertinacity, yet no instance is upon record where disease had ever been communicated through that channel, even when purification had been omitted.

In this enlightened age, when science has revealed so many remedial secrets, when the materia medica has a range and power never before known, when anatomy, physiology, and pathology have assumed the highest rank in the arts of preserving health and life, it may well be considered whether it be not just, as well as safe, to abandon the more onerous of these restrictions which in the darkness of the early ages prevailed in relation to diseases supposed to be contagious.

Commerce, which is the handmaid of science, has a right to insist on a modification of these antiquated opinions, and to enlist in her favor the scientific discoveries of the age. It is believed that while proper restrictions may be placed on what is actually dangerous, as expressed by the term *fomites*, there should be a complete relaxation of restrictive rules in other respects.

The persons of the sick and the well, should be relieved from the confined and impure atmosphere of the vessel, and instead of being imprisoned within the narrow limits of a Quarantine station, they should at once, after proper cleansing and changing of raiment, be allowed free egress into the pure air of the country, or to their customary places of residence.

The question of safety in regard to clothing and bedding, and articles of merchandise which, by medical advice, are brought under the term of *fomites*, is a different one, and must be treated with a due regard to the lights which science and experience have granted to us.

In entering upon this investigation, the Committee deemed it to be their duty, before attempting to arrive at any definite conclusions in regard to the scientific points involved, to invite the attendance at their meetings of a number of the most eminent members of the medical profession in our city, with the view to elicit their opinions on the several questions under examination.

The invitations were promptly and cheerfully responded to; and the Committee have now to return their cordial acknowledgments to the following gentlemen, namely—

Dr. ALEXANDER H. STEVENS,
Dr. JOHN W. STERLING,
Dr. ALFRED C. POST,
Dr. ELISHA HARRIS,
Dr. ALEXANDER N. GUNN, Health Officer,
Dr. JEDEDIAH MILLER, Health Commissioner,

for the able, scientific, and disinterested counsel given by them to the Committee in the course of the examination of the subjects treated herein.

The opinions of these gentlemen, so far as they were committed to writing by themselves, will form a part of the Appendix to this Report.

In reply to certain questions prepared by the Health Commissioner, in reference to the Quarantine practice to be observed in certain cases, written communications were received from Dr. Miller, Dr. Stevens, Dr. Harris, and in part from Dr. Sterling.

Certain general questions of the Committee, in regard to the use and efficiency of floating hospitals at Quarantine, are replied to by Dr. Harris.

A valuable paper was also submitted by Dr. Sterling, on the subject of Wet Docks in connection with Quarantine.

The oral testimony and explanations given before the Committee, a sketch of which was taken by one of their number, embrace many interesting suggestions.

These papers and the recorded testimony, will be found to contain a mass of useful information, the result of scientific research and long experience in medical pursuits, which deserves and will justify the public confidence. The statements of facts and the opinions founded thereon, are entitled to a careful consideration.

In referring briefly to the general purport of this testimony, it is proper to remark that all the eminent practitioners before the Committee united in the general sentiment, as to the unnecessarily restrictive regulations hitherto adopted in maintaining the Quarantine at this port.

The Health Officer and the Health Commissioner were frank and liberal in the construction given by them to the official engagements under which they were about to be called on to act; and the Committee have every reason to believe that so far as the action of these officers is concerned in the administration of existing laws, the public interests will not suffer from any avoidable restraints or burdens.

While it is warmly contended by the latter officer, Dr. Miller, that the existence of a restrictive system of Quarantine in regard to vessels and cargoes, has been mainly instrumental in preserving the city from the invasion of infectious epidemics for a number of years past, yet he with equal frankness and candor concedes the propriety of remitting the restraints upon passengers and crews, on vessels resting under suspicion of yellow fever.

This concession from an experienced and intelligent officer of the Department, charged with administrative duties under it, is an important step of progress in the right direction. The removal of Quarantine restrictions from the persons of the sick and the well, except temporarily in extreme cases, will greatly relieve the over-taxed interests of Commerce, and give much greater freedom to its energies in the future.

It will now be necessary to consider how far existing restrictions should be modified in regard to crews and passengers sick, or in danger of infection, from small-pox, typhus fever, or cholera. In reference to the first-named disease, it is unfortunately almost always rife in our midst; and the regulations of Quarantine can do no more for the protection of the community against its ravages, than to keep the well who pass through its bounds, free from danger of contagion, by vacciuation, and to place the sick at the earliest practicable moment, within the influence of good air and judicious treatment. For these objects, institutions admirably arranged and managed, are established under the municipal government, and can be resorted to at an hour's notice.

Typhus fever is a malady to be dreaded, and under certain unfavorable circumstances more so than either of the diseases mentioned. In unwholesome places, and especially in uncleanly and infected vessels, it is a fearful enemy of human life. It should rarely, if ever, be confined within the close bounds of a Quarantine station, longer than is indispensably necessary for the purification of person and clothing and the removal to more appropriate accommodations.

The like remarks will apply to cholera, in regard to which disorder confinement should rarely be resorted to. This is a malady to be found only where localizing conditions, that favor its prevalence, exist, as on shipboard, in filthy dwellings, in pestilent atmospheres, or where large bodies of people are congregated. How palpable then is the truth, that the patient should at once be removed beyond such influences!

This fearful disease, though comparatively new to us on this continent, is well understood by scientific men, who do not regard it in any sense as bearing the character of contagion, save only under particularly unfavorable circumstances in regard to locality and surrounding influences. Surely for such a malady a better refuge should be provided than is to be found at a Quarantine station.

Where, then, is the policy, the necessity, or the humanity, of confining the unfortunate objects afflicted by such disorders, within a narrow, crowded, perhaps infected station on land, or on the decks of a floating hospital, riding at anchor on the stormy waters of a distant bay? Is it to be believed that the sick can be restored with greater certainty, at less expense, or with less sacrifice of comfort or convenience, under the charge of Quarantine officers, than with their friends, under medical treatment, frequently of their own choice and, always in this community, of the highest order of talent, and with the beneficial influences of home, change of scene, and domestic quiet, surrounding their beds of suffering?

If these reflections are just in regard to the sick, they apply with additional force to the well; who have been hitherto subjected to all the evils of a restrictive Quarantine, but in regard to whom it is now believed a more judicious policy has been adopted and will hereafter prevail.

These are questions deserving of the serious consideration of the public authorities; but it is believed by the Committee that this is not the proper occasion for their further discussion. It should be remarked, however, that the adoption of floating hospitals for the accommodation of the sick at Quarantine is an experiment only defensible on the ground of absolute necessity. If properly constructed, with all the aids that science can give in securing abundance of pure air, perfect cleanliness, and a proper temperature, such vessels might be used with safety in the quiet waters of a sheltered bay; but the Committee have serious apprehensions that inconvenience, discomfort, and possibly danger, may result from the resort to such accommodations in a more exposed situation.

As a temporary resource, however, in a critical emergency, the Committee cannot do otherwise than justify the action of the Commissioners of Quarantine in respect to the floating hospital. The necessity for the adoption of such an alternative has grown out of the difficulties attending the present (or former) Quarantine location. The question is yet to be solved whether the shores of two States, accessible from our waters, are to be permanently withheld from the public service, in the exigencies of a great public necessity, on the mere grounds of private interest and personal prejudice, or whether a better and a wiser judgment shall prevail in the future.

In closing their discussion under the second branch of the questions referred to them, the Committee are of opinion that the effect of the general prevalence of the doctrine of non-contagion, founded as it is on principles of truth, justice, and philanthropy, as adopted by the National Convention, will be beneficial in an eminent degree, to the interests of commerce, and that it will exercise a large influence in extending the work of reform in other branches of the Quarantine system.

And in this connection the Committee recommend that the Chamber shall earnestly apply itself to the duty of obtaining the proper legislation, providing for a thorough revision of the Quarantine laws at the next session of the legislature; and that active efforts be also made to obtain national legislation authorizing the establishment of proper warehouses in some convenient location, for receiving goods and merchandise from vessels undergoing Quarantine.

Under the third head, that relating to the question of lighterage and other services connected therewith, the Committee have carefully examined the facts connected with the abuses practiced during the last and former Quarantine seasons, and decided to use all the influence within their control to break down the principle of monopoly which had been introduced into that business.

On presenting this question to the notice of the Health Officer and Health Commissioner, then present with the Committee, both readily admitted their willingness to open the business to a free competition, and to receive proposals from all parties engaged in such duties, who were proven to be responsible and capable. In concert with these parties, the Committee prepared a tariff of charges for lighterage, which was agreed to by all who had expressed a desire to enter into the competition; and at the request of the Mayor of the city, acting as President of the Board of Health, it was submitted for his information, accompanied by the following letter from the Chairman of this committee :

CHAMBER OF COMMERCE,
New York, May 27, 1859.

To Hon. Daniel F. Tiemann :

SIR :—In accordance with your request, I have the honor to hand you herewith a memorandum of prices established by the Quarantine Committee, for Lighterage from Quarantine to this city. In establishing this tariff, the Committee have heard the principal parties engaged in the lighterage business, before them, and the rates have been fixed with great care, and will no doubt be satisfactory to all parties.

The Committee, in submitting their report, would suggest that in their opinion the interest of the merchant would be promoted by allowing all parties of a respectable and reliable character to engage in the business under such rules as the Health Officer may direct.

With great respect, your obedient servant,

(Signed,) THOMAS TILESTON,
Chairman of the Quarantine Committee.

The tariff alluded to will be found in the Appendix.

The principle of free trade in Lighterage, as in other branches of trade and commerce, should be insisted on by the Chamber as far as it can rightfully exercise power and influence on this question. The actual power is vested in the Health Officer, and he is officially connected with the Board of Health. This tribunal, therefore, has the control of the whole subject, and can exercise that power under existing laws, according to its own sense of duty and interest.

All that the Chamber can do at this time, is to insist on the principle, and to hold the authorities to a rigid accountability to public sentiment for any deviation they may make from so just a principle and self-evident a duty.

While engaged in the discussion of this subject of Lighterage, the question arose as to the liability of the owners of lighters for loss on cargoes in transit between vessels at Quarantine and the docks of the city. Owners of lighters present at the meeting of the Committee entertained different views in regard to the liabilities imposed on them, and also, as to the resort that should be had to the insurance policy under such cases. The Committee deemed it advisable, therefore, to refer the question to the Board of Underwriters; and the following reply from that body places the question in a light which may need some action of the Chamber:

OFFICE OF THE BOARD OF UNDERWRITERS,
New York, May 25, 1859.

Gentlemen :—At a meeting of the Marine Insurance Companies of New York held at this office yesterday, the following preamble and resolution were adopted, viz.:

Whereas, A communication has been received from a Committee from the Chamber of Commerce, on the subject of Lighterage,

Resolved, That the Underwriters of this city will appoint an Inspector of Lighters, and for an additional premium of one quarter per cent. they will cover all risks on merchandise insured by them respectively, from quarantine grounds within Sandy Hook to this city, that may be placed on such lighters as may have the certificate of said Inspector; and that the liability of the lighter shall be the same as that of a vessel under a marine policy.

(From the Minutes.)

G. S. STAGG,
Clerk of the Board.

To Messrs. THOS. TILESTON and WM. NELSON, *of the Committee of the Chamber of Commerce.*

The Committee are of opinion that the policy attaches to the cargo from the time it is received on board the vessel until it is landed in the city. If the Underwriters dissent from this judgment, and think that the transhipment to a lighter terminates the risk under the policy, then it is of the highest consequence, for the owners of cargoes thus situated, to know the fact, and to take measures to determine where the risk shall devolve. The Committee, therefore, submit this question for the further action of the Chamber, with the remark that in fixing the tariff of rates for lighterage, they assumed the fact that the owners of lighters should be held responsible in cases of loss, until this question should be definitely settled.

In conclusion, the Committee regret the necessity which has led them to trespass at such inordinate length on the time and attention of the Chamber. The subject referred to them has long been regarded as one of deep interest and solicitude to this community, whose main subsistence is derived from commerce. They have supposed that a full and frank discussion might lead to a better understanding of the merits of the controversy, and possibly to such legislation as would remove some of the prominent evils which render the present system so burdensome to the citizen, and so injurious to the character of our port as a favorite haven of commerce.

In accordance with the views herein stated, the following Resolutions are presented for the consideration and action of the Chamber.

Respectfully submitted,

NEW YORK, June 29, 1859.

(Signed)

    T. TILESTON,
    P. PERIT,
    ROYAL PHELPS,
    F. A. CONKLING,
    PROSPER M. WETMORE,
    C. H. MARSHALL,
    WILLIAM NELSON,
    GEORGE OPDYKE,
    F. M. FRENCH,
    DRAKE MILLS.

Resolutions submitted by the Select Committee on Quarantine.

I. *Resolved,* As the sense of the Chamber of Commerce, that the Quarantine Regulations of this port, so far as they concern the preservation of health and life, may safely be modified; and that, so far as the interests of commerce are involved, they ought to be modified and amended in the following particulars, viz.:

1. To provide for the free egress of healthy passengers and crews from vessels detained for examination, subject only to proper personal purification and changes of raiment.

2. To insure a more liberal construction of the laws in regard to the detention of vessels supposed to be infected, and the release of all not proven to be so within the period of five days.

3. A reduction in the charges of Quarantine in every branch of the system where they are now found to be exorbitant and burdensome, to a standard more just and equitable.

4. The selection, at the earliest period practicable of a permanent location, within the waters of New York, for a Quarantine Station adapted to the public exigencies.

II. *Resolved,* That the Chamber will urge upon the legislature of this State at its next ensuing session, the passage of a law providing for the adoption of the before-mentioned principles in the regulations and restrictions of the Quarantine system at this port.

III. *Resolved,* That the Chamber will memorialize the Congress of the United States for the establishment of a system of warehousing in connection with the Quarantine Station of the port of New York.

APPENDIX.

---◆---

A. I.

QUESTIONS OF THE COMMITTEE.

CHAMBER OF COMMERCE,
NEW YORK, *May* 23d, 1859.

ALEX. H. STEVENS, M. D.

Dear Sir,—The Chamber of Commerce, having appointed a Committee to examine into the present system of our Quarantine regulations, I take the liberty to ask from you a reply to the following questions :—

What restrictions, if any, should be placed on passengers or others, arriving from infected ports?

Also on baggage, and the necessary purification?

Also on merchandise of a hazardous character, and on that considered not hazardous? and what process or length of time may be considered requisite for the purification of merchandise?

The Committee are anxious to discharge the important duties confided to them, and by all means protect the city from the introduction of any pestilential disease that can be avoided; at the same time it is perfectly obvious that no unnecessary obstruction should impair the commerce of this great city.

With great respect I remain,

Your most obed't servant,

(Signed) THOS. TILESTON,

Chairman.

A. II.

QUESTIONS SUBMITTED BY DR. MILLER, Health Commissioner.

1. Would you deem it safe for vessels, from parts where yellow fever prevailed, having had no cases of fever amongst their crews while in their ports of departure, or on their passage, or after arrival in port with a passage of not less than ten days, arriving between 1st day of April and 1st day of November, to proceed at once to the wharves of the city?

2. If exceptions are to be made, with what cargo, and under what circumstances, should they take place?

3. What disposition would you make of vessels and cargo, having had yellow fever while in their ports of departure, or during their passage, or after arrival in port?

4. Personal Quarantine is not required for yellow fever in this port; do you deem it necessary for small-pox?

5. If cotton is discharged at Quarantine, would you permit it to be lightered to the city at once?

6. To what shall we attribute the exemption of New York from yellow fever for the past thirty-seven years?

7. Would sugar in boxes or casks be proper cargo to lighter direct to the city from an infected ship?

B. I.

ANSWERS BY DR. STEVENS, AND NOTES OF HIS TESTIMONY.

NEW YORK, 24 *May*, 1859.

Dear Sir,—In reply to your inquiry as to "what restriction if any should be placed on passengers and others, coming from infected [yellow fever] ports." I answer *none whatever*, if they take a bath, or otherwise undergo due ablutions, and come away with new clothing, or their own properly purified, and leave their baggage behind until that also is duly purified.

The second query relates to the purification of "baggage." In many cases I have no doubt simple exposure of personal baggage to the wind and sun for a few days, as house-wives treat their bedding, would be amply sufficient. But it would be hazardous to trust to such means when the vessel in which they have arrived has been long in a sickly and especially a tropical port, and has had sickness on board.

The third query relates to "merchandise of a hazardous character, and that not considered hazardous, and the length of time considered requisite for its purification." On these points I must decline giving any positive opinions. I am not aware that our Quarantine establishment has made any record of the facts upon which alone a positive opinion could be founded; for the experience of other ports in different latitudes is not, precisely and in all cases, applicable to that of New York.

With great respect,

I am truly yours,

ALEX. H. STEVENS.

To T. TILESTON, ESQ.,
     Chairman of the Quarantine Committee of the Chamber of Commerce.

ANSWERS TO DR. MILLER'S QUESTIONS.

1. A long passage, with the hatches kept closed, does not at all render a vessel less liable to communicate yellow fever, but rather the contrary, especially if sailing in warm latitudes. But the health of the

crew and the continued ventilation of the ship during the passage, afford a presumption in favor of the healthfulness of the vessel, but not necessarily of every part of the vessel. In all cases I should deem it right to have the bilge water pumped out and replaced by other water until, after twenty-four hours, it came up tolerably pure; and then under favorable circumstances I should judge there would be little or no danger in letting her come to one of the wharves of the city. What I should explain as favorable circumstances are the extra-tropical position of the port of departure, shortness of the time the vessel has remained there, the cleanliness of the wharf and neighborhood where she is to land, and low degree of heat of the season, as well as the nature of the cargo itself. I would further require the vessel to be thoroughly ventilated, and treated as to the bilge-water process above described at least three times a day.

2. Cotton coming from Charleston and taken on board-ship from a *healthy part of the city*, I should infer would not acquire any dangerous properties, if it did not remain more than one week at any of the wharves of that port.

3. I would not allow them to approach the city or any thickly inhabited place, until after discharge of cargo and thorough purification.

4. I would follow the Boston system, which has proved entirely successful.

5. Refer to 2.

6. I attribute it to the better drainage, underground sewerage, Croton water, and the removal of many thousands of privies and cesspools; in part also to Quarantine, and some unknown causes.

7. I should not deem it entirely safe until the city and wharves are made thorough clean and kept so. When this is done I do not doubt that the quarantine, as against yellow fever, typhus fever, and cholera, may be greatly relaxed.

I submit these replies rather as contributions to the subject,—imperfect, but not I trust erroneous in principle.

I am, &c.,

A. H. STEVENS.

New York, 26 *May*, 1859.

NOTES OF EVIDENCE GIVEN BY DR. ALEX. H. STEVENS BEFORE A COMMITTEE OF THE CHAMBER OF COMMERCE, N. Y., MAY 20, 1859.

The yellow fever may be considered a native of certain latitudes; but north of Charleston, a germ is required to produce the disease.

A peculiarity of the disease is that its *radius* is regularly and gradually enlarged; it does not skip from one place to another.

There can be no doubt, that the disease has been communicated by infected baggage. The length of time required to properly ventilate and disinfect baggage, is a question of great uncertainty and difficulty.

Would suggest that matters of detail be passed over by the Chamber, and that the attention of this body be directed to devising, and putting in operation, a new and improved system of quarantine. Approves and has long advocated the plan of floating hospitals for yellow fever, small-pox, cholera, typhus-fever, &c. Yellow fever is destroyed by a temperature of 32° of Fahrenheit's Thermometer. The germ of typhus-fever is destroyed by a high degree of heat, say 250° of the same scale. In Boston only a single case of small-pox occurred last year.

Expressed the opinion that the health-officer, and all under him, should be paid a stated salary, and that it should be made penal by statute to accept any fee whatever. The attention of the health-officer should be given entirely to the discharge of his professional duties ; consequently he should have nothing to do with commercial transactions.

B. II.

GENERAL REPLY OF DR. HARRIS.

That Yellow Fever has frequently been spread from place to place and propagated by means of ships arriving from places in which that fever was at the time prevailing epidemically, is a fact universally acknowledged by all persons familiar with the history of that disease, and competent to judge properly of the evidence in such cases.

Whatever may be the doubts and the unsettled questions respecting the precise mode in which such propagation of the fever may be effected, it is an undisputed fact that vessels while remaining in infected ports have, in repeated instances, become so infected as to communicate the Yellow Fever from, and by means of, the various compartments of the ship, even when emptied of all cargo and divested of movable furniture. It also has been observed that the peculiar cause or infection of Yellow Fever in such vessels remains most persistently and in the greatest activity in the lowest compartments or spaces, and the closest, filthiest, and dampest portions of the ship.

The questions relating to the property or power of retaining and transmitting the infection or cause of Yellow Fever by means of cargoes and material substances that have been conveyed from infected ships or from other infected places, though not settled upon so indisputable a basis as the questions relating to the infection or contamination of particular parts of a ship, have, nevertheless, been decided with a great degree of certainty by multiplied observations, as regards certain classes or kinds of materials and packages. So far as the present state of medical knowledge relative to this subject extends, it seems to warrant the opinion that the infectious cause of Yellow Fever is prone to inhere or remain in and be conveyed by any packages, spaces, apartments, porous or absorbent materials and textile fabrics, that *retain and closely confine the atmospheric air and other gases ;* and that the liability of such packages, spaces, or materials, to convey and communicate the virus or cause of Yellow Fever, is greatly enhanced by special impurities, dampness, and a temperature so elevated as to promote organic growth and decomposition.

These are facts, whatever may be the proper theory to account for them. Therefore, it cannot truly be stated that " vessels arriving from infected ports, having had no cases of fever amongst their crews while at their ports of departure, or while on their passage, or after arrival in port, with a passage of not less than ten days," would not, under certain atmospheric conditions, be *liable* to propagate Yellow Fever in the city of New York, if allowed to proceed at once to the wharves and discharge their cargoes in the city. Therefore, I cannot conscientiously answer Dr. Miller's *first* question affirmatively, except with the explanations and distinctions here indicated.

It should be borne in mind that, taken by itself alone, the simple circumstance of no case of Yellow Fever having occurred among the crews and passengers of vessels from infected ports,—as mentioned in the first question, would not of itself by any means establish the fact that such vessels or their cargoes would not be liable to propagate the fever when unloading or lying at the wharves of the city. In repeated instances has Yellow Fever been propagated by such vessels and their cargoes at the wharves of this city, as well as to lightermen, stevedores, and other persons in the vicinity of such vessels when discharging cargo at the Quarantine anchorage.

The striking characteristic of Yellow Fever first made known in this country by Dr. John W. Francis, that it seldom or never attacks the same person a second time,—in other words, that the first attack of the fever is *protective,* as in the case of small-pox,—has been demonstrated by later observations. It is also a fact, that by a protracted residence in, or frequent voyaging to, a tropical climate, persons may become so acclimatized or seasoned as not to be readily susceptible to the causes of the fever. Many vessels arrive at this port with crews and passengers so protected or seasoned as to withstand the operation of the causes of the fever that may at the time exist within the vessels. Hence, it is obvious that in such instances the non-occurrence of cases of the malady on board, as referred to in the question, would not furnish conclusive evidence of the non-infection of such vessels. It is true, however, that there might occur instances in which the non-appearance of cases of yellow fever on board a vessel that had cleared from an infected port, might furnish very strong presumptive evidence that the ship and its cargo would, under no circumstances, communicate the fever; and were suitable attention given to the storage and condition of cargoes, and to the cleanliness and condition of vessels clearing from unhealthy ports, and were such vessels provided with the necessary means of efficient and forcible ventilation, and the preservation of a dry and cool atmosphere in all parts of the ship, it is probable that they would seldom, perhaps never, require the interposition of any quarantine restrictions for the protection of the public health.

As it will require many years for the principles and facts of sanitary science to obtain such hold upon the public mind as would be necessary to effect a proper control over those nautical and commercial arrangements which now permit the presence of yellow-fever infection or its causes on board ships, as well to remove and prevent all the localizing or predisposing conditions and causes that may favor the propagation of yellow fever in our midst; and as it is possible that some doubt and uncertainty may always exist relative to the actual sanitary condition of a certain proportion of the vessels arriving from very sickly ports,—the interests of commerce no less than the safety of the public health would seem to demand that suitable warehouses should be provided at some insulated locality in the bay of New York, where all vessels that are really *liable* to communicate yellow fever may at once discharge their cargoes, and without unnecessary delay re-load and proceed to sea.

The delay of such improved and much-needed facilities will necessarily expose the city to danger from yellow fever, or continue to inflict needless and heavy burdens upon commerce.

The present system of lighterage and temporary detention of vessels in Quarantine, affords at best but a very imperfect degree of sanitary protection against yellow fever.

Had the high temperature and humidity that prevailed in this city in 1795, 1798, 1799, 1803, and 1822, characterized the summers and autumns of 1856 and 1858, the cities of New York and Brooklyn would inevitably have been swept by pestilence, notwithstanding the oppressive quarantine system then in operation.

The accumulated observations and experience relative to the propagation of yellow fever in the port and city of New York during the last sixty years, as well as the corroborative and almost unanimous testimony of all the best medical observers of this malady in other parts of the world, force upon my mind the conviction that we cannot safely, without exceptions, answer the Committee's first question in the affirmative; and, further, that the rules and practices to be established in accordance with rational and truthful answers to the *second question*, viz., " With what cargo, and under what circumstances should exceptions be made," should and may be such as to secure greater protection to the public health, and at the same time relieve commerce of many needless burdens that are incidental to the existing regulations of Quarantine.

A properly stated reply to that *second* query would involve all the more important facts relating to the propagation and spread of yellow fever; and in order to answer it properly in regard to the great variety of cases that are likely to come before the officers of Health, it would be necessary to know and define the real nature and condition of the cargo, the circumstances attending its delivery and storage on board the ship, as well as its previous storage and care in port, the topography and character of that port, the treatment of the cargo, and of the hold and all other compartments of the vessel, during the voyage—particularly as respects the degree of ventilation which had been secured, the conditions of temperature, dryness, cleanliness or uncleanliness, together with the personal history and physical characteristics of all the persons on board such vessels, and their habits, whereabouts, and management while on the voyage.

The reasons and the necessity for instituting such investigations, are obvious; and complicated and difficult as such investigations might sometimes be found, we are warranted in the opinion that in a very large majority of the cases defined under Dr. Miller's *third query*, as well as most of the arrivals defined in the *first*, a suitable investigation would enable the officers of Health to decide with certainty the question of infection or non-infection, and that commerce would thereby be at once relieved of more than half the burdens hitherto inflicted by our quarantine regulations relative to yellow fever.

We know that some of our Health officers have been in the habit of instituting very careful inquiries on some of the foregoing points, but there has not been any reliable and thorough system adopted by means of which the proper accuracy could be secured in such investigations. In the present state of our Quarantine system, it would greatly promote the public interests and facilitate commercial transactions if our National Government, through the Department of State, would authorize and put in force an efficient system of special inquiries to be made and certified by its consular or commercial agents, or its customs officers, in every port in which yellow fever is liable to prevail;—such inquiries to respect all the conditions and circumstances of the ship at the port of clearance, the cargo, crew, and passengers; as regards the various circumstances to be designated in the inquiries by which it would be possible to judge of the probability of the contamination of the vessel or cargo,—including, of course, direct categorical replies relative to the port of clearance.

To insure proper protection to the public health, and greater facilities to commerce, such a system should be immediately proposed by our officers of Health, and authorized and *enforced* by the general Government, so that during the sickly season in tropical ports, the peculiar advantages of such inquiries might be enjoyed at the port of New York, the certified replies to which should be brought by and demanded of every ship-master.

It will be observed that in the general terms of the preceding statements, I have answered the *second*, and the *third*, as well as the *first* of the Committee's questions. But, for the purpose of giving my replies that practical definiteness and applicability which the Chamber of Commerce may desire, and in order to answer succinctly the several queries proposed by the Committee respecting vessels and cargoes that have been exposed to the causes of yellow fever, I beg leave to submit the following synopsis of the facts and principles bearing upon those questions. This, I trust, may be more satisfactory and practical than direct categorical replies, which, from the statement of the questions themselves, would not admit of direct replies that would not be justly open to criticism and confutation.

The first attack of yellow fever in any person usually proves perfectly protective for several years, or for a lifetime as in the case of small-pox.

Protracted exposure in, or frequent voyaging to, tropical regions, renders most persons, so exposed, less liable than others to contract yellow fever.

The peculiar cause or infection of yellow fever tends to the lowest compartments of a ship; or, more definitely, that infection is liable to be accumulated and retained only in the closed compartments of a ship. It is known that the upper decks and main cabins of an infected vessel may be so free from infection, when well ventilated, that even the most susceptible persons may fail to contract the fever, if exposed to none of the apartments or the cargo below.

A large majority of the cases of yellow fever that occur on board vessels while remaining at infected ports, or while on their passage from such ports to New York, result from the exposure which such persons have encountered while in the sickly port of departure, and not from infection on the ship.

The infectious cause or virus of yellow fever is prone to inhere or remain in, and to be conveyed by, any packages, spaces, and apartments, porus and absorbent materials, and textile fabrics, that *retain* and closely confine air and other gases; and the liability of such packages, spaces, and materials to convey and propagate that fever, is greatly enhanced by *special impurities, moisture,* and a temperature so elevated as to promote organic growth and decomposition.

The occurrence or non-occurrence of cases of yellow fever on board ships from infected ports, unless occurring after the seventh day from the date of departure from the infected locality, could not, of itself, be regarded as determining, or even as indicating, a proper decision of the question of infection or non-infection of such vessels.

Inasmuch as most vessels departing from places in which yellow fever is prevailing epidemically, are necessarily exposed to certain liabilities to become infected, the *exceptions* in favor of allowing *free pratique* to particular vessels or classes of vessels at our Quarantine station, should be based upon those conditions only which are known to prevent the contamination of ships and their cargoes from the epidemic cause or infection of the fever, unless positive evidence can be at once produced, establishing the fact, or at least, the strongest presumptive proof, that particular vessels and cargoes are not so contaminated.

The most reliable of direct evidences of non-infection in any vessel or cargo would be—

1st. That no cases of yellow fever had occurred on board, after the sixth or seventh day out from the infected port, notwithstanding the fact that several of the ship's company or crew were known to be susceptible to the fever, and had been freely exposed in the stowage and care of cargo, or had otherwise been exposed in the lower and closer compartments of the vessel; the existence of general cleanliness and freshness in all parts of the ship and cargo, the absence of dampness and decomposition and of offensive bilge water, and the presence and operation of an effective system of ventilation.

A vessel that could present such a sanitary bill, or, if having an acclimatized and protected ship's company, could present all other than the first item of evidence, could, with comparative safety, be permitted to come directly to the wharves of the city at any time after the sixth or seventh day out from her port of clearance.

Other exceptions than those just detailed, would seem to be warranted upon the following conditions :—

1st. A vessel, having on board only such persons as had been protected from the fever by previous attack, or by long seasoning, might safely proceed to the city with her cargo, as in the last-mentioned instances, provided that cargo did not consist of substances that are prone to retain confined air ; or—consisting of such porous materials,—it were ascertained that they had not been deposited or exposed in any infected locality, the ship itself having been but slightly exposed to such localities, having taken in cargo by lighters or otherwise, when lying far out in the stream, or otherwise removed entirely beyond any infected place ; and particularly if the sugar, cotton, and other suspected materials, had come directly from plantations, without storage in a sickly port.

2d. In most instances in which, whatever the cargo, a vessel twenty-five days from a sickly port, with good ventilation, careful attention to cleanliness, the absence of offensive bilge water, or any filthy places, there having occurred no new cases of fever after the first ten days of that period, provided that some of the unprotected and unseasoned persons of the ship's company, who had been much exposed in the lower and least ventilated portions of the ship, still remained unaffected by fever.

Finally, it may be stated that all vessels from places where yellow fever prevails at the time only endemically, and in a particular section in which neither the ship nor her cargo had been exposed, as usually is the case in all our United States ports, except New Orleans and Galveston, may safely be permitted to proceed directly to the wharves of the city, at any period subsequent to the tenth day from departure from the sickly port, provided no cases of the fever appeared on board during all that period.

Generally, as regards sugar and molasses, it would be safe to permit them to the city without delay, provided that in the case of such cargo from badly infected ports or from ships known or believed to be infected, the packages were first subjected to perfect aëration for two days, or to a forced and thorough ventilation for an hour or two. But without such precautions, we are not warranted in asserting that, in such instances of suspected contamination, it would positively be safe to transmit such packages directly to the city.

ELISHA HARRIS, M.D.

No. 253 Fourth Avenue,
  June 1, 1859.

NOTE.

It will be observed that in the foregoing statements some prominence is given to the fact that the propagating cause of yellow fever is liable to be conveyed from place to place by means of any materials or agencies that retain or closely confine and convey considerable quantities of atmospheric air from an infected locality. This is only a general statement of fact relative to the agencies by which yellow fever is spread from places, in ordinary commercial intercourse. In the present state of medical knowledge, it would be impossible to give a perfect definition to the propagating or infectious cause of yellow fever, further than the existence and operations of that cause are ascertained to be associated and connected with, or dependent upon, certain known and recognized conditions of atmospheric air, and the special *fomites* or materials by which the air and the infection are conveyed from infected localities.

The question whether a *distinct* virus or appreciable miasm exists as the cause of yellow fever has not been, and may never be, absolutely determined. Whatever the essential nature of this infection may be, it certainly is essentially *specific*, and different from all other infections. Facts clearly warrant the opinion that the atmospheric air is invariably the vehicle or medium for the transportation of the infectious cause of yellow fever, and that a tropical temperature and considerable moisture are conditions essential to the reproduction and epidemic operation of the infection. The evidences upon this subject are both direct and circumstantial.

It has always been observed that this infection has a marked preference for humid places and wet materials, and that water, particularly when stagnant, seems to possess the property of absorbing, retaining, and imparting it;—the fever poison is not destroyed by water at ordinary temperatures.

There exists no evidence that any of those material substances and *organic bodies* which possess the property of immediately decomposing the chemical constitution of the atmospheric air which they may imbibe or retain, ever have conveyed the infectious cause of yellow fever from place to place. No evidence exists in support of the hypothesis that the human body, of itself, has ever communicated the fever; nor is there any reason to believe that its propagating cause has ever been reproduced or generated in or by the human body. This is a striking peculiarity of the propagating and infectious cause of the fever; as all other exotic or transportable infections seem to be capable of re-production and perpetuation by the living human system. This absolute disparity in the recognized analogies of yellow fever with the other transportable infections, has given origin to interminable disputations among medical theorists; but, as stated by Humboldt, the vomito has never been *known* to be personally contagious in a single instance.

The true characteristics of a disease cannot be established by analogical and hypothetical speculations. Especially is this true respecting yellow fever, as the facts relating to its history and characteristics conclusively demonstrate that *its* propagating infectious cause is peculiarly *self-existent*, and in no wise dependent upon, or affected by, the human body so far as its generation, reproduction, and diffusion are concerned; and that while it may fatally affect the human system by inducing in it that disease known as yellow fever, the actual cause or agent which induces the fever does not seem to be in any manner affected or increased by the persons who suffer from its effects.

In my replies to the queries proposed by Dr. Miller, through your Committee, it has been found impracticable, in the brief limits assigned, to enter upon detailed statements relative to processes and means for the proper disinfection of materials contaminated with the virus of fever, or to state the varied and important exceptions that may properly be made in favor of particular articles of merchandise that are now liable to Quarantine. But we may state generally,—that when once the infectious cause of yellow fever has obtained such foothold or point of operation as to infect an entire house or ship, or a particular district, the fever is very sure to continue to propagate itself in that particular locality during a period which, if not terminated by frost, ceases only after long-continued and drying winds, great storms, or a long-continued low temperature; and, secondly,—that so great is the tenacity and so marked the localization of the infection, that no ordinary winds and natural ventilation, nor even the temporary application of water at ordinary temperatures, or the immersion of infected materials, or the scuttling of the hold of an infected vessel, will remove the infection with certainty.

In closing this hastily prepared summary of the facts relating to the peculiarities of the propagating or infectious cause of yellow fever, I beg leave again to allude to the vast importance of invoking the aid of the National Government for the relief of commerce from many of the unnecessary burdens and inconveniences which are incident to the present defective regulations of quarantine in this and other Atlantic ports.

The National Government not only might properly provide the essential requisites for our quarantine establishment, viz., the necessary *warehouses and docks*, but by its sanction and authority alone can a proper system of sanitary inquiries and health bills be provided for, and made, at the various ports where yellow fever is liable to prevail.

E. H.

B, III.

ANSWERS, BY DR. STERLING.

No. 144 West 40th Street, New York,
May 28, 1859.

J. Smith Homans, Esq.;
 Cor. Sec. Chamber of Commerce.

Sir,—I respectfully present the following answers to the Interrogatories of Dr. Miller:

1. It would be prudent to ventilate the hold for three days; after which I would deem it safe, under the circumstances noted, for the vessel to proceed to the city.

2. I do not consider it possible for cargoes of merchandise, whether raw or fabricated material, in a sound state, to communicate febrile disease, or disease of any kind. A cargo of decaying fruit or vegetable matter might contaminate the atmosphere to a small extent, and consequently should not be landed on our wharves in hot weather. I do not believe, however, that they would originate yellow fever; otherwise we would have it in the vicinity of Washington Market every summer. In such instances as last specified, the hold of the vessel should be left open and well ventilated for three or four days after its contents are ejected.

3. The vessel should be detained at Quarantine until thoroughly expurgated; and to facilitate this process, the goods should be landed.

4. The sick with yellow fever should be sent to a hospital *on land*, at least for humanity's sake. The sick with small-pox should be landed

and sent to their appropriate hospital. The well should not be detained after their garments and baggage are washed and ventilated. In addition, it would be advisable to vaccinate those who are susceptible, and let them proceed on their journey.

You cannot Quarantine small-pox. It stalks through our city every day. Almost every day I see it, except in midsummer and the depths of winter, when it is less rife. But the sick who arrive with it must be provided with a suitable asylum on the land, where they can be properly taken care of. I have admitted into Marine Hospital, from shipping at Quarantine, fifty or more cases of this loathsome disease in one day, and as many as thirty from a single ship. Congregate such numbers with this disease on board of hulks, and the ratio of mortality would be very great. Small-pox patients require plenty of space, as well as plenty of air. Cool air, cold water, sparing diet, cleanliness, as far as is practicable, and good attendance and nursing, are almost all they require for their cure. It is a great misfortune that hospitals are not provided in the suburbs of our city, to which small-pox patients might be sent. I have known great suffering result from the delay consequent upon sending them down to Marine Hospital from the city, and probably with additional risk of life through loss of time.

The great prophylactic—vaccination—is preferable to Quarantine restrictions; but the Germans, in their own country, in spite of their coercive laws, seem to have frequently neglected it. From this nation we derive the greater number of small-pox patients; very few, comparatively, from other nations are admitted from Quarantine into Marine Hospital with this disease.

5. Yes.

6. Humanly speaking, we cannot satisfactorily account for the exemption of New York from yellow fever during the past thirty-seven years, any more than we can explain the change which has occurred in the type of inflammatory and febrile diseases generally, as well as in their treatment, during that period. The lancet, which was then used most liberally, is now almost discarded from practice; and total abstinence in fevers has yielded to more liberal diet. My belief is, that whenever yellow fever has prevailed in the city of New York epidemically, the grand source has been of domestic origin, though this may have been roused into action by a foreign cause, easily assigned but not readily proved. This is theory. Individual cases of this disease, few and far apart, present themselves in this city every year, but do not extend. This is fact. Much of this exemption, however, may be attributed to the substitution of other pestilences, which have taken off the material by a forty-fold mortality; and again, to our increased domestic comforts, far surpassing those of thirty-seven years ago. The introduction of the Croton water into our city, by affording a bountiful supply of a refreshing and healthful beverage, promoting cleanliness of person and of domicile, and sometimes of our streets, has without doubt contributed greatly to its salubrity, especially in those localities where its use most frequently prevails.

7. I can see no objection. I do not believe that sugar, though packed in boxes tacked together with small strips of hide, introduced

the yellow fever at the foot of Rector Street. Sugar of itself is a powerful antiseptic; and hides abound in every condition and variety in the Swamp*—a locality notorious for its salubrity and exemption from epidemic diseases.

Respectfully submitted,

JNO. W. STERLING.

My answer to Dr. Miller's fifth Interrogatory "If cotton is discharged at Quarantine, would you permit it to be lightered to the city at once?" was briefly "Yes."

Unwilling to occupy too much of the time of the Committee of the Chamber of Commerce, I entered into no explanation. I therefore beg leave to occupy a little of your attention while I assign my reasons for this answer.

Quarantine assumes that articles of commerce, whether of the raw or manufactured material, are capable of absorbing or imbibing pestilential virus, and that thereby epidemic diseases are conveyed from one country to another. Among the articles supposed to be peculiarly adapted for the absorption of this poison are wool, woolen and linen cloths, cotton, furs, hair, ostrich feathers, dry hides, rags, sponges, vellum, all kinds of paper, tallow candles on account of their wick, animals with wool or long hair, and what not. These articles were required to undergo purification, and this was a tedious process. Sometimes even forty days were occupied in its performance, and in foreign lazarettos there was a staff of officers especially designated for this purpose.

I will describe the process of expurgating wool.

Wool to be taken out of bags, and ranged in heaps not above four feet high. These were all moved twice a day, turned, and the heaps mixed by the porters, with their hands and arms bare, during forty days successively; and every five days, besides the usual labor, moved out of the place they were in. (HOWARD *on Lazarettos.*) Now, we must admit that the only proof of a pestilential virus in an article is, that it actually produces disease, and that the first action of this virus, if it really existed, would be on those who are immediately, directly, and persistently exposed to it; and consequently, the persons occupied in performing the process of expurgation would be the first subjects of disease. What does experience prove on this point? That at no season of any year, in any country, has a single officer, or operative, whose business it is to open and expurgate goods, been known to be attacked by pestilence, or by any other form of disease which has been surmised to be imported or of foreign origin.

From official reports from Rochester, Portsmouth, Falmouth, Milford, Bristol, and Hull, received by a Committee of the House of Commons, G. B., 1849, the following testimony was derived:

John Green, Esq., testifies—That he has never known any person who handled goods in Quarantine to be infected. Mr. Saunders, Superintendent of Quarantine at Standgate Creek, testifies—Every illness,

---

* That portion of the city of New York where the hide and leather trade is carried on.

however slight, is reported and brought under my notice. Does not recollect a single instance in which the expurgators, who are the persons who examine goods, have been taken ill in consequence of such examination. During the fourteen years he has been Superintendent, does not recollect a single instance. Mr. Nichols bears similar testimony. No infection in people employed in unpacking and repacking. Sir Gilbert Blane says—" If no instance has occurred of any such expurgator being infected, there can be but little risk of infection, and therefore little benefit in that mode of airing, which frequently materially damages goods." Ralph Green, Esq., Inspector of Hospitals—Is not aware that he has ever heard of any instance in which the expurgators, or any of the persons employed in unpacking and repacking goods in this country (G. B.), have been affected. Mr. W. Matthias, Superintendent of Quarantine at Milford Haven, and Dr. Newberry, Medical Superintendent of Standgate Creek, give similar testimony. Giovanni Garcini, who was employed twenty-nine years at the Lazaretto at Malta, on being asked " Have you ever known an instance of the persons employed at the Lazaretto in exposing cotton, wool, feathers, flax, rags, sails, or other susceptible articles from infected places, to have been attacked with the plague whilst so employed, excepting vessels having the plague on board ?" replied " Never." Dr. Laidlaw also stated to the Committee that he had availed himself of every opportunity of making inquiry as to this point among the officers of all the Quarantine stations in all foreign countries visited by him, and that he never found even a reputed or suspected case of infection among this class of persons, nor had any one examined by him ever heard of such instance.

For further testimony on this point, as well as for the particulars of exemption from infection during the examination and expurgation of 31,000 bales of goods brought from Alexandria into Great Britain in the year 1835, when it is computed that 200,000 of the inhabitants of Egypt fell victims to the plague, I beg leave to refer to the Report of the General Board of Health on Quarantine, as drawn up and presented to both Houses of Parliament in 1849, &c.

Furthermore, we find in the *Encyclographie des Sciences Med.*, tom. xvi., Nov., 1843, the following testimony of Mons. Aubert, in his paper on the Reform of Quarantine, presented to the Acad. Roy. de Med. de Paris :

Mons. Aubert affirms, as the result of his observations in the East, that during a period of one hundred and twenty-four years (from 1717 to 1841), 64 vessels only, returning from the East to Europe, had plague on board; and that no instance has occurred of the porters or guards of the merchandise being attacked with the plague. Bales of merchandise, *sent from pestilential foci*, whether opened upon deck or in Lazaretto, have never produced the plague,—and that during a period of one hundred and twenty-four years.

I am under the impression that many of our obnoxious Quarantine regulations, with regard to merchandise especially, have been derived from those of foreign countries without due investigation. In 1665, London was ravaged by the plague, supposed to have been introduced by goods imported from the East.* This supposition is now regarded as groundless. Previously to that time London was visited by plague once in twenty years. In 1666 it was thoroughly purified by fire; and a new order of things induced a salutary change. Since then it has been exempt from this malady. On equally plausible grounds it

---

* "During the plague of 1835," says Dr. Laidlaw. "which preserved its epidemic character from the beginning of January till the commencement of June, and during which period upwards of 9.000 persons in the town of Alexandria (it is computed that 200.000 persons fell victims to the disease in the whole of Egypt within this period of time) alone must have suffered from the disease, vast quantities of cotton wool were embarked on board of British merchant vessels and sent to England. *The cotton so embarked was taken from the government cotton stores, where the plague raged most fearfully;* it was pressed on board the English vessels, so as to render it convenient for storage, by the crews, assisted by working parties of Arabs, who came from the shore and returned home to sleep. There was nothing like a Quarantine observed by any of the English captains; and the English sailors were constantly at work at the cotton-store, shipping off the bales in their boats. In fact, there was the most perfect communication and contact which any reasonable experimenter could have desired; and no precautions, no fumigations, no airings, were adopted. The cotton was stowed away in the holds of the ships, screwed into as small a compass as possible, the hatches closed; and thus it was conveyed to England. In some of the ships the plague broke out among the crews during the time they were lading; but the work of stowing the cotton went on notwithstanding. Communication between the infected ships and those which had no sickness on board was unrestricted; and the disease did not spread to any extent among the former, nor was it communicated apparently to the latter.

"The exportation of cotton wool from Alexandria during the year 1835 amounted to 98.502 bales, all of which was sent to Europe in the following proportions: to England, 31,709 bales; to Marseilles, 33,812; to Trieste, 32,362; to Leghorn, 424; to Holland, 150; to sundry parts, 45. An English bale of cotton generally consists of about 200 lbs. weight.

"The English vessels which cleared out from Alexandria during this year of epidemic plague were twenty-five in number, which carried into Great Britain no less than 31,000 bales of goods supposed to be capable of contamination in the highest degree. Of these twenty-five ships, eight actually had the disease among their crews during the time they were loading. All these vessels when they arrived in England had to perform a long Quarantine, for the supposed purpose of purifying the cotton from the latent *fomites* it was supposed to contain. If the Quarantine officers did their duty, all of these bales of cotton should have been ripped open and freely handled, first by the crew, and afterwards by porters and other persons appointed for such duties in the presence of a Quarantine Guardian; and if no persons were attacked during this expurgation, and after a period of forty days or more, according to circumstances, the ship's company were entitled to *pratique* (liberation from Quarantine).

"By orders of Council, cap. xxxii, it is regulated that all bales of cotton shall be opened from end to end, from one end to the other, and so much taken out as to leave room for handling daily the interior of the bale. But this is not in all places fully attended to. In Ireland, however, whether the vessel arrives with a clean or a foul bill of health, there appears to be no airing of the cargo. They rarely do more than hoist the bale of cotton on deck, &c.; and a bale of cotton is not opened at any time. It is evident, then, that were it possible for plague to be communicated by cotton, this disease must constantly break out in Ireland, where cotton as much impregnated with plague virus as is possible, is sent amongst the manufacturers without the slightest precaution; nor could the imperfect airing which cargoes undergo at other Quarantine stations prevent Manchester from becoming the seat of plague."—*Extract from Report on Quarantine, by the General Board of Health, presented to both Houses of Parliament by command of her Majesty. London,* 1849.

has been affirmed that the yellow fever has been imported into our city, in one or more instances, by merchandise; and the circumstantial evidence is certainly very strong in proof thereof. But by no means so strong as the numerous testimonials advanced above of a contradictory character; for I presume this testimony will apply with equal propriety, if not much greater force, to yellow fever, admitted to be of far less contagious character than the plague. Be this as it may, while I consider that sound merchandise cannot introduce yellow fever, and consequently should be admitted to market immediately, I would prohibit that which is contained in foul envelopes from admission, until cleansed or new-cased. This is not only a sound sanitary measure, but also would induce captains of vessels to take good care of their freight, if they do not wish to be detained. Decaying material, whether animal or vegetable, should be discarded, &c.

Very respectfully submitted
By your obedient servant,

JNO. W. STERLING.

B. IV.

ANSWERS TO QUESTIONS, DY DR. MILLER.

1. Not in all cases.

2. If the vessel is clean, and the account of cargo obtained from the officer of the vessel satisfactory, the use of windsails, and a detention of three to five days for observation, principally for the purpose of allowing an opportunity for the health-officer to be confirmed in his opinion, and especially if she uses the patent ventilation now in use on Nelson's vessels,—under these circumstances, and the usual West-India cargo, I would allow such vessel to discharge at the dock, notwithstanding she comes from an infected port. If the reverse of this appeared upon inquiry, she should be compelled to discharge at Quarantine. The cargo in most cases may be lightered direct to the city.

3. Usually they should discharge at Quarantine, cleanse and purify, when, no one becoming sick from working on board, the vessel may with safety be allowed to proceed to the city, and take in cargo, &c. Yet upon investigating, if it should be satisfactorily shown, that the disease was contracted *on shore* while in port, her cargo and condition being of the same character as that of answer No. 2, she might be permitted after observation of three to five days to proceed to the city and discharge. But cases occurring on her voyage, six or seven days out of port, or after or near arrival, are indications making it necessary for her to be compelled to discharge at Quarantine; she may then cleanse and purify, and proceed to the wharf for freight.

I would allow this short detention, after being discharged, cleansed, and purified, because I have no facts to show that the discharged vessel will impart the infection, except to those who visit her below decks, the miasm being heavier than common air.

A vessel discharged at Quarantine, cleansed and purified, I take to be in a different condition from one arriving in ballast, with sickness especially, if the laborers shall have been exempt from disease during and following her discharge. This *fact* will be important to establish the safety of her proceeding to the city after discharging.

4. I deem the present system of vaccination at Quarantine as sufficient and ample, so far as passengers arriving at this port are concerned; I presume no port with the same class and amount of emigration has much less of small-pox, than the city of New York. A hospital may as properly be located on Wards' Island as on Blackwells'.

When the same class of population, with the same intelligence, as is to be found in Boston or Providence resides in this city, we may then expect the same exemption from small-pox, and not probably before. I am prone to believe, that ignorance has much more to do with the prevalence of this disease than want of more summary laws.

I would allow passengers exposed to small-pox, on being vaccinated, to proceed without detention.

5. Cotton is often brought from the country by railroad or steamboat, and transhipped at once to this port. If the account of the cotton should establish this fact, it being also in good condition, it might properly be lightered at once to the city.

But if in bad condition, and long stored in an infected district of the port from which shipped, it should not be permitted in the city before November. Investigations and inquiries carefully made in this manner will enable us to make a proper and safe discrimination; and at the same time relieve commerce from any unnecessary expenses and delays.

6. To what shall we attribute the exemption of New York from yellow fever for the past thirty-seven years? I believe that an efficiently managed Quarantine has had much to do with the exemption of New York from yellow fever. The late Dr. Alexander F. Vache in his letter to the Legislative Committee of 1845, says:—" Let it be remembered, that yellow fever has not appeared in this city for nearly a quarter of a century, and not since the present health-laws have been rigidly enforced; therefore, let us not forget in our zeal for innovation and improvement the good old maxim, 'let well enough alone.' Admit they are (the health laws) in a measure restrictive to commerce, and bothersome to the merchant, will any calm observer deny they are alike protective of his life and conducive to his interests? The pecuniary loss of a hundred years by the Quarantine establishment, cannot equal the ruin and devastation of a single year of the pestilence. Who does not shudder at the memory of closed dwellings, the suspension of business, the shunned city, the Quarantine abroad, and the sepulchres of hundreds, during the summer of 1822?" I trust that medical gentlemen who believe to the contrary, will give us a *practical* and satisfactory plan, by which the necessity of a rigid Quarantine for infected vessels and cargoes may be obviated or diminished. The laws relating to Quarantine give full power to the "Commissioners of Health," to grant all

relief to vessels and cargo they may deem prudent, with a proper regard to the health of the city. Underground drainage, and Croton water may have something to do with the non-appearance of the epidemic; yet we had but little of this previous to 1845; and our docks and ships would appear to be in many places well adapted to the planting of yellow fever, even at this day. I am quite sure, the experience of sixty years will show the immunity of New York from this epidemic to be due to our Quarantine system. It may have been *oppressive*. If it can be prudently modified, I am quite sure the authorities having charge of this duty would be happy to aid in such a desirable result. The experience of every health-officer, as well as physicians to the Marine Hospital, has led to the same conclusion in relation to our Quarantine laws and their execution. Dr. Joseph Bailey, then health-officer, says in a communication to Mayor Allen in 1822:—I cannot suffer this opportunity to pass without expressing my firm conviction, that rigid Quarantine regulations are essentially necessary to guard the inhabitants of our commercial cities against the introduction of pestilential and infectious diseases."

I must, therefore, again express my unbounded conviction both from *facts* and *theory*, that New York is indebted to our Quarantine system for her exemption from yellow fever for the past thirty-seven years.

. 7. In most cases, I should deem it safe and proper to lighter casks or boxes of sugar direct to the city.

B. V.

REPLY OF DR. HARRIS IN REGARD TO FLOATING HOSPITALS.

We are warranted in the opinion that Floating Hospitals for the treatment of febrile and pestilential diseases must necessarily be inferior in many respects to hospitals on land, and that when anchored in tidal currents and exposed to the open sea and the force of the winds, the disadvantages of such hospitals would be very great; yet we incline to the opinion that floating hospitals in the bay of New York may be made valuable auxiliaries to the Quarantine establishment of this port, until a suitable location shall have been secured for the necessary hospital buildings upon *terra firma*. But we should regard the substitution of a floating hospital for hospital accommodations on the land, as justifiable only upon the ground of expediency, for temporary purposes; and if resorted to, they should be anchored in the most quiet and insulated locality that can be found within two miles of the Quarantine anchorage; and the Hospital Ship should be so fitted up and furnished as to provide for perfect ventilation and cleanliness, from the upper decks to the very bottom of the keelson.

ELISHA HARRIS.

NEW YORK, *June* 1, 1859.

B. VI.

SYNOPSIS OF ORAL TESTIMONY GIVEN BEFORE THE COMMITTEE AT THE SEVERAL MEETINGS HELD AT THE CHAMBER.

Present—DRS. STEVENS, STERLING, POST, MILLER, GUNN, AND HARRIS.

The questions propounded by the Committee being under consideration, Dr. STEVENS was of opinion that no detention was necessary in regard to passengers on board vessels from yellow-fever ports. The baggage should be properly purified by exposure to the air. Merchandise, coming under the term *fomites*, required time for purification.

DR. STERLING gave oral answers to the questions of the Committee, which he subsequently reduced to writing, as follows :—

I do not consider that yellow fever is communicable from person to person. It does not, like small-pox, produce its similitude. If patients with yellow fever are divested of fomites, they can be landed at once without jeopardizing others. They should be removed to clean, properly equipped, and well ventilated apartments on land, and not be confined to other vessels. The transfer of the sick from one vessel to another must produce a greater depression of their spirits than if they were removed to an agreeable tenement on shore, where they would also be less exposed to agitation of the body.

Passengers who are well, should not be detained at Quarantine after their clothing, bedding, and baggage have been thoroughly cleansed by washing and purified by exposure to the open air.

I believe that the garments, bedding, and baggage from an impure and infected vessel, are powerfully efficient in exciting the disease. Next to the hold of a foul ship, they are the most fertile source of the disease ; but neither will communicate the disease at a remote distance, or cause its extensive propagation, or to assume the character of an epidemic, unless the atmosphere into which they are introduced possesses a congenial disposition, susceptible of assuming by impregnation, inoculation, or fermentation, that peculiar constitution which exists where the yellow fever is endemic.

I have never known an instance in which the beds or bedding, in the wards of the Marine, have communicated the yellow fever to nurses or other attendants,—attention to cleanliness in removing all impurities, and thorough ventilation, being strictly regarded.

I have ascertained, from personal observation, that the washing of the clothes of yellow-fever patients brought from ships infected with yellow fever, has induced this disease. During the autumn of 1848, while this disease prevailed at Marine Hospital, four of the washerwomen were attacked, and two of them died with black vomit. The steward and his wife, into whose sitting-room the effluvia from the wash-house penetrated with an highly offensive odor, were seized with yellow fever. The steward died ; the wife recovered. I was also informed that the wife of a mate of one of the sickly vessels, who died at Stapleton with this fever, took the disease after washing his clothes, and died likewise. A rag-carpet manufacturer, at Tompkinsville, slept upon some refuse articles of clothing which he picked up floating from vessels lying at Quarantine, and fell a victim to yellow fever.

JOHN W. STERLING.

DR. ALFRED C. POST concurs substantially with the other gentlemen who have given their testimony. The clothing, the hair, and perhaps some other parts of the person, may possibly communicate the disease. There is reason to believe that diseases are sometimes communicated by means of miasms adhering to the hair, especially in the case of women who wear long hair. It would therefore appear to be a wise precaution to take special pains in cleansing the hair. As to the purification of baggage, it may be accomplished by a freezing temperature, kept up for some time. Bedding and other thick articles should be destroyed, or carried away to a cold *climate*. Baggage may be buried, or otherwise disposed of, until winter, when it should be freely exposed to frost, after which it becomes entirely innocuous. An instance occurred in this city some years ago, in which a trunk of clothes had been sent from New Orleans while the yellow fever was raging in that city. It was kept through the winter without being opened, in the garret of a house, where it was not exposed to cold. In the spring, a lady opened the trunk and took out the clothes. Soon afterwards she was taken sick with yellow fever, and the attack proved fatal. The witness does not believe that the disease is contagious, or that it is communicated by any poison generated in the body of the sick person.

DR. MILLER, in reply to the first inquiry of the Committee, said that personal quarantine is not required in this port. Dr. Vaché, in his book, stated that as long ago as 1845 he advocated the abandonment of quarantine for persons. Practice of the last season. Personal quarantine abandoned at the close of the last season. Practical inquiries submitted to the Board of Health. Personal quarantine not required at present, and the practice respecting baggage in accordance with the views here expressed by the medical gentlemen.

DR. GUNN (the health-officer) expressed his concurrence in the views stated by the gentlemen who have spoken. Propounded a series of questions prepared by himself and his deputy. (These queries were not handed by Dr. Gunn to the Committee.)

DR. ELISHA HARRIS expresses his concurrence in the replies made by Dr. Stevens Believes that the question of the effect of this hypothetic *virus*. There is no question of the fact that there is no risk from the person. All the English and French writers who have been consulted by him concur. The cases which are reported in the books and which seem to be in conflict with this view, admit of a different explanation. The minds of medical men, when disinterested, are all brought to this conclusion.

The case of Rio Janeiro. The disease made its appearance and has continued ever since. The physicians there are all agreed that it is not communicable. The opinions of the profession in New Orleans have undergone a great change. The process of washing is used, but the importance of it is apt to be overrated. No case of a person bringing the disease with him from a vessel. Has known many cases at fifty where persons have come from ships in a tolerably cleanly condition, but never one where the disease was communicated.

The exigencies of commerce do not admit of a detention until frost.

In 1856, baggage washed or steamed at a high heat, some garments spread upon the ground during two afternoons, and then gathered up and put into chests. Has never known any injury to result.

Yellow fever has never become epidemic, in any locality, under circumstances which would lead to the conclusion that it has come from persons and their baggage. A considerable quantity of the *virus* is required to spread the disease.

Dr. Stevens would suggest that practical experiments be made for the purpose of distinguishing the seeds of infection; would be willing to superintend the experiment.

Dr. Harris referred to the experiments made in Berlin for the purpose of distinguishing the fomites of puerperal fever at Berlin temperature of 170° of Fahrenheit's thermometer. Consulted Prof. Reid, of Edinburgh, and that gentleman has the subject under consideration. Practice at Quarantine in subjecting clothing to a boiling heat.

C. I.

RECORD OF PROCEEDINGS OF NATIONAL CONVENTION.

NATIONAL QUARANTINE AND SANITARY CONVENTION,

College of Physicians and Surgeons,

NEW YORK, April 30, 1859.

Ordered, That the Secretary be authorized to publish the record of the resolution of A. H. Stevens, M. D., and the votes thereon, as adopted at the preceding session of this Convention :

Resolved, That, in the absence of any evidence establishing the conclusion that yellow fever has ever been conveyed by one person to another, it is the opinion of this Convention, that personal quarantine of cases of yellow fever may be safely abolished;

Provided, That *fomites* of every kind be rigidly restricted.

AFFIRMATIVE, 85.

The President, J. H. Griscom, M. D., of New York.
A. H. Stevens, M. D., of New York.
E. Harris, " "
Stephen Smith, " "
D. B. Reid, " "
A. S. Jones, " "
J. S. Cooper, " "
S. T. Hubbard, " "
H. D. Bulkley, " "
A. Underhill, " "
Wm. Rockwell, " "
J. Miller, " "
Wm. H. Williams, " "
H. Guernsey, " "
Jas. R. Wood, " "
Frank Tuthill, " "
John Watson, " "
J. McNulty, " "
W. C. Anderson, " "
J. W. Sterling, " "
S. S. Purple, " "
Joel Foster, " "
Jas. D. Pond, " "
T. W. Johnston, " "
T. C. Finnell, " "
E. Lee Jones, " "
Samuel Boyd, " "
J. H. Jerome, " "
W. R. Donaghe, " "
A. N. Bell, " "
J. C. Hutchinson, " "
F. E. Mather, Esq. "
Chas. H. Haswell, " "
J. P. Batchelder, " "
P. M. Wetmore, " "
C. C. Savage, " "
H. O'Reilly, " "
Wm. Nelson, " "
Jos. Blunt, " "
Geo. B. Wood, M. D., Pennsylvania.
R. La Roche, " "
J. F. Lamb, " "

L. W. Buffington, M. D., Pennsylvania.
U. A. Piper, " "
H. G. Clark, " Massachusetts.
J. M. Moriarty, " "
D. H. Storer, " "
Hon. F. W. Lincton, Jr., "
S. D. Craven, Esq., "
Geo. A. Curtis, " "
Jos. S. Bailey, " "
T. C. Amory, Jr., " "
Silas Pierce, " "
Geo. Dennis, " "
Ebert Atkins, " "
Clement Willis, " "
J. A. Nichols, M. D., New Jersey.
M. Baldwin, " "
S. J. Southard, " "
J. B. Trimble, " "
H. D. Holt, " "
Gabriel Grant, " "
S. A. Cross, " "
E. T. Wittingham, " "
J. M. Cormelison, " "
C. F. J. Lehback, " "
G. W. Cowdery, " Virginia.
W. M. Wilson, " "
J. H. Henderson, Esq., "
Conway Whittle, " "
Wm. M. Kemp, M. D., Maine.
D. J. McKew, " "
J. Gilman, " "
C. B. Guthrie, " Tennessee.
J. F. Wilson, " Delaware.
John Darby, " Alabama.
C. F. Force, " D. Columbia.
E M. Snow, " R. Island.
Jos. Mauran, " "
F. H. Peckham, " "
J. F. Callan, Esq., D. Columbia.
Wm. L. Bladen, Esq., Pennsylvania.
W. McPhail, " Missouri.
Hon. D. S. Gregory, New Jersey.
Hon. M. Bigelow, "

NEGATIVE, 6.

J. W. Francis, M. D., of New York.
S. B. Halliday, Esq., "
E. R. Nichols, M. D., New Jersey.

H. A. Parkhurst, Esq., New Jersey.
Wm. H. Taylor, " Pennsylvania.
Thos. H. Town, " "

(Extract from the Minutes of the Convention.)

(Signed,)   CHARLES H. HASWELL,
A. W. BELL, M. D.,
GABRIEL GRANT, M. D., } SECRETARIES.
HENRY G. CLARK, M. D.,
ELI D. HINKLE, M. D.,
H. ST. CLAIR ASH, M. D.,

C. II.

TARIFF OF CHARGES FOR LIGHTERAGE, MAY, 1859.

Articles.	Quantity.	From the Lower Bay.	From the Quarantine.
Coffee	per bag	$0 12½	$0 07
Cotton	" bale	50	28
Flour	" barrel	15	9
Grain	" bushel	4½	3
"	" sack	10	6
Hides, wet	Each	8	4
Hides, dry	Each	4	2
Lead	per ton	1 75	1 00
Logwood	"	1 63	1 25
Mahogany	"	1 63	1 25
Molasses	per hogshead	1 00	60
"	" barrel	38	25
Provisions	" barrel	20	13
Rags	" bale	1 00	50
Segars	" thousand	10	5
Sugar	" hogshead	1 00	60
"	" tierce	75	40
"	" barrel	25	13
"	" box	35	20
Tobacco	" hogshead	1 63	1 00½
"	" bale	25	12
Wool	" "	1 00	45
Molasses	per tierce	75	40
Provisions	" "	25	15
Skins	" dozen	4	..

C. III.

SUPPLEMENTARY NOTE BY DR. STERLING.

I have had an opportunity for becoming conversant with yellow fever, having served at the Quarantine hospital as assistant physician during the year 1848, when this disease prevailed at Staten Island to an alarming extent. It was evidently derived from vessels having the yellow fever on board. During the summer and autumn of 1848, many transports arrived from Vera Cruz, at the close of the Mexican war, with sick soldiers on board, laboring under camp dysentery and other formidable diseases, as well as vessels from other ports, (in the aggregate 44,) where the yellow fever is rife during the season. These vessels rode at anchor in the middle of the stream. At the period when the yellow fever appeared at Staten Island, fifteen vessels were lying in the Quarantine roadstead from New Orleans, Vera Cruz, and St. Domingo, on board of most of which a number of cases of yellow fever had occurred from which the disease undoubtedly originated. From these vessels thirty-seven cases of yellow fever, and one hundred and ninety of bilious remittent fever were admitted into the Marine Hospital. Of the former twelve, and of the latter twenty, died. But the disease was not confined to the hospital. It appeared first among the boatsmen of the revenue department, and of the health-officer's barge; and almost simultaneously several persons, whose business exposed them at Quarantine, were affected; and the disease extended along the eastern shore of Staten Island, involving the towns of Tompkinsville and Stapleton. The number of sick averred to be of yellow fever without the walls of the hospital was one hundred and fifty, of which number thirty died. (See Report of Committee on Quarantine to the Legislature in 1849, Doc. 60, Dr. Whiting's testimony). The heat of summer had been great and protracted, and the weather rather dry. In the vicinity of Stapleton is a place called Rocky Hollow, which during the summer and autumn was a complete quagmire; sending forth volumes of marsh miasmata to contaminate the atmosphere, and which, doubtless, rendered it susceptible of assimilating with the foul atmosphere from the vessels. This deterioration of the atmosphere, of whatever kind or nature it may have been, rendered it unwholesome at an earlier period; and it was remarked that, previously to the occurrence of the yellow fever there was much sickness and mortality among the canine species in this locality. Since then Rocky Hollow has been filled up, and a drain constantly flowing carries off its superfluous moisture rapidly to the harbor. Although yellow fever has since repeatedly visited Quarantine to an alarming extent, Stapleton has escaped its further visitation.

The pernicious atmosphere, however, was not restricted to Staten Island. I heard of much severe sickness at Bergen Point. A seaman named Chas. Swanson was brought from a vessel outward bound, (to James' River,) which vessel had not then reached the boundaries of Quarantine; he was admitted into the hospital as a case of bilious remittent fever, and died with black vomit on the 11th of October. The yellow fever prevailed at Staten Island from the 19th of August to the 21st October, 1848.

The following instance seems to indicate that the germ *fomites* or *materies morbi* of yellow fever may be conveyed in baggage-cars from one sickly place to a remote distance; and that by means of baggage the yellow fever was carried in cars almost air-tight from Mobile to Citronelle. This disease appeared at Citronelle about the 16th of August, 1853, about one month after the first case of yellow fever appeared at Mobile; and sixteen out of eighteen of the employees on the railroad, besides many laborers, died of it. The distance between Mobile and Citronelle is thirty-two miles, and the population of the latter town about three hundred, out of which number one seventeenth ($\frac{1}{17}$th) died. A Committee appointed at Mobile to inquire into the origin of the disease at Citronelle was informed on what was considered a sufficient and satisfactory authority, that those first attacked at Citronelle were persons engaged in unloading the baggage-cars which has been kept closed from Mobile, a distance of thirty miles. (See Report of Committee on the Sanitary Condition of New Orleans, published in 1853, and D. J. C. Simond's Report on Quarantine.) But even admitting that the disease originated from the baggage, had no other cause existed for the extension of it, it would have become extinct with the individuals who inhaled the poison from the cars. It should be borne in mind also that Citronelle was a village of but twelve months' growth, that railroads had been or were being excavated in this place and its immediate vicinity, so that there must have been an extensive disturbance of the soil, a fruitful source for emanation of the yellow fever poison, and that without such disturbance the disease would not have raged there epidemically.

I do not conceive it possible for the *materies morbi* adherent to baggage, raiment, or bedding to radiate to a remote distance without undergoing so much dilution in the atmosphere as to render it innocuous. The deleterious effects of these emanations, like those from the hold of a foul ship, are generally restricted to and expended upon those who approximate them closely. They cannot produce an epidemic unless the atmosphere with which they commingle is congenial, susceptible of being changed in its constitution by being impregnated with the poisonous effluvia evolved from the articles, and thereby receiving that impression which assimilates it to the peculiar atmosphere where yellow fever is epidemic.

J. W. STERLING.

C. IV.

EXTRACT FROM A PAPER READ BEFORE THE ACADEMY OF MEDICINE, JUNE 1st, 1859, BY JOHN W. STERLING, M. D.

"Whoever has observed the uneasy manner in which vessels ride at anchor in the Lower Bay, agitated, and tossed to and fro, by the swell of the waves, even under a moderate breeze, may appreciate, not only, the danger to which such vessels are exposed during tempestuous weather, but also the difficulty of transferring their goods to lighters along side. Be the anchorage grounds ever so safe, the Lower Bay, from the extensive and unobstructed sweep of the north-easterly and westerly winds over its broad expanse, is by no means commodious for vessels there compelled to ride out their thirty days' Quarantine; and, consequently, if better shelter and protection be not provided for them during their detention, such vessels will hereafter seek a safer port, and besides, their officers, by giving to it a bad name, will deter others from entering our harbor, especially during the quarantine season.

In order to afford better shelter and protection, a Breakwater has been suggested; but, in my humble opinion, it would not answer the purpose so well as a *Wet Dock*, and, besides, it would be more expensive.* In Wet Docks vessels would lie safely inclosed, and could discharge their cargoes on the wharf along side, on which warehouses or piazzas might be erected for the reception of goods, until the foul ships which brought them are thoroughly expurgated, or the goods be permitted to enter the market. (See Howard's plan of the Lazaret'o San Leopoldo, at L ghorn. "Account of the Principal Lazarettos in Europe, 4to, 2d edition. London, 1791.")

Inasmuch as those vessels which bring the Yellow Fever into our port draw less water than our European Packet Ships, and propellers of a light draught are in a great measure superseding them, a depth of eighteen feet of water, which, I have been informed, can be readily found in the Lower Bay, will be sufficient for the Docks in question, and, if capable of receiving thirty vessels at a time, by the sides of the wharves, will be capacious enough for every needful purpose. For I feel persuaded, in my own mind, that if the unlading and expurgation of vessels be promptly and methodically attended to, instead of being detained thirty, it would require no more than eight days for discharging cargo and thorough purification. So that refitting, relading, and clearance of vessels (especially if there be likewise an Export Dock for the reception of goods sent from the city,) would be expedited rather than delayed by proper Quarantine regulations.

"That the construction of *Wet Docks* has done much to facilitate and attract commerce is an historical fact, and, in addition to their convenience, afford better protection to property while vessels are unlading. Previously to the introduction of Wet Docks on the Thames, the property annually pillaged from vessels was estimated to amount to £500,000 sterling; though McCulloch, from whose Commercial Dictionary, I quote, considers this estimate somewhat exaggerated. The first Wet Dock in Great Britain was constructed in Liverpool, about the year 1708, at which time Liverpool was but an inconsiderable town. This however, was the commencement of her mercantile importance, and the accommodation afforded by her docks is one of the circumstances that has most strongly conduced to her extraordinary increase in commerce, popula-

---

* According to the testimony of Richard Delafield, Major of Engineers, before a Committee of the Legislature, January, 1847, we perceive—That up to January 1837, the Delaware Breakwater had cost $1,630,000, and he considers that not much less would suffice for a similar structure in Sandy Hook Bay—and further, he says—"A Breakwater has no tendency to protect a vessel from the force of the winds; their fury and power in driving vessels from their moorings is the same with as without a Breakwater. It is only in resisting the force of the waves and heavy seas, that such a structure is of any service."

tion, and wealth." Her docks now inclose an area exceeding 90 acres of water.

"The West India Docks were the first constructed in the Thames. They were commenced in February, 1800, and partially opened in 1802. The Export Dock is 870 yards long by 135 wide. Its area about 25 acres. The Import Dock is of equal length and 166 yards wide. The South Dock, which is appropriated both to import and export vessels, is 1183 yards long, the locks at each end are 45 feet wide, large enough to admit ships of 1200 tons. At the highest tides, the depth of water in the docks is 24 feet, and the whole will contain with ease 600 vessels of from 250 to 500 tons. There are other docks pertaining to this department, which, together with the above, and the warehouses, included an area of about 295 acres.

This spacious and magnificent structure was formed by subscription, and vested in the West India Dock Company. Their capital being £1,380,000 sterling. It has proved a profitable as well as a beneficial investment. In addition to the West India Docks, there are, on the Thames, the East India, London, and St. Catharine Docks. For more minute details, see McCulloch's Commercial Dictionary.

But these Docks are on a much grander and more expensive scale than would be required for a Quarantine establishment. Being intended for Yellow-Fever ships only, a Dock capable of conveniently accommodating thirty vessels alongside the wharves, would be sufficiently capacious; for after discharging cargo, they could haul off into the middle of the basin for expurgation. I thus judge from the testimony of Dr. Whiting, ex-health-officer of this port, as recorded in Doc. 60 of Assembly, in 1849, wherein he states—

That the number of sickly vessels at Quarantine (during one of the most sickly terms at Marine Hospital) from the 13th March, 1848, to January 1st, 1849—a period of $9\frac{1}{2}$ months, was—

> with Yellow Fever, 44
> Bilious Remit't " 62
> Ship " 135
> Small-Pox, 42
> ———
> 283.

From this statement, I judge that it will not be necessary to send more than thirty vessels into Dock at one time, and the prospect is that, in consequence of our Quarantine restrictions, the number of vessels arriving from Southern ports and the West Indies will be materially reduced during the ensuing Yellow-Fever season. After the Quarantine season is over, these Docks might be used as a rendezvous for vessels driven into our port by stress of weather, and for supply vessels, &c., for vessels in distress on the coast, &c., &c., which humanity will dictate.

I would also suggest that a *Dry Dock* be constructed in immediate contiguity with the wet dock, as very foul ships, especially if they contain bilge water, leak more or less, and require overhauling. Besides, I am under the impression that the chief difficulty of eradicating the poison from a Yellow-Fever ship, by any process hitherto devised, short of frost, may be attributed to the moisture which exists in the deepest part of the vessel, and which, while the bottom lies several feet below the surface of the water, it is difficult to evaporate. This moisture holds the poison in solution, and as the moisture exhales from heat, the poison of course will be carried up with it, and when condensed by cold, the poison will be precipitated with it. This appears to me to be a rational theory. Now, if the vessel be elevated completely out of the water on a warm cloudless day, while the seams are being caulked, and the solar rays beaming with power upon the hull of the vessel, the moisture will evaporate, carrying up with it the poison, which will soon be diffused in the atmosphere, and, by dilution, rendered harmless. Or else by careening the vessel from side to side, the poison which lurks in the deepest recesses of the hold, and, unless rarified by heat, is specifically heavier than the superincumbent air, will thereby be dislodged and expelled; after which, sweeping, ventilation, and white-washing, will complete the purgative process. And all accomplished without occupying more time than the recaulking of the vessel may require.

But it may be said, such contrivances will cost a great deal of money. I presume they will also save a great deal of money, and doubtless of time, which is worth quite as much. But there is no doubt all the cost can be met without calling upon the State for pecuniary aid :—

1st. By a levy on Richmond County, for riotous destruction of valuable property, in the sacking and burning of Marine Hospital, at Staten Island.

2d. By the proceeds of Sale of Quarantine grounds.

3d. By calling upon the United States for an appropriation, in proportion to Revenue collected in port of New York, as compared with other Ports in the United States, for the purpose of constructing a Marine Hospital. It is very evident that, unless we desire to abolish our Quarantine system, we will have to reconstruct the entire establishment, for it cannot be expected that Hulks or Floating Hospitals will be more than a temporary expedient. That the citizens of New York have a just claim upon the United States Government for an appropriation to erect a Marine Hospital, I will now endeavor to show.

According to the Report of the Hon. Jas. Guthrie, Secretary of the United States Treasury, for the Fiscal year ending June 30th, 1856, it appears that the Government has appropriated the following amount, $1,987,861.91, or nearly two millions of dollars, for the site and erection of Marine Hospitals throughout the Union. Of this amount, there have been appropriated to

New Orleans,	$436,459 20.
San Francisco,	224,000 00.
Chelsea, Mass.,	150,000 00.
Cincinnati,	136,000 00.
St. Louis, Mo.,	118,574 00.
Detroit, Mich.,	105,500 00.
and to 16 other States the balance,	817,828 71.
	1,987,861 91.

While no appropriation for a similar purpose seems to have been made to the State of New York.

In addition thereunto, the United States Government has paid out of the Seamen's Fund, for medical attendance upon Seamen, and other contingent expenses, and in many of the above-named Hospitals, he gross amount of $310,160 81, while it has received from Seamen, for the Benefit of said Fund, $153,945 65.

The following statement shows the amount paid into this Fund, and also that received from the United States only.

	Amount paid into Fund.	Amount rec'd from the U. S.
New York	$44,551 65	$28,456 58.
California	8,912 34	48,774 07.
Massachusetts	18,739 94	26,304 23.
Louisiana	14,930 72	20,455 38.
Illinois	2,143 78	18,791 07.
	$44,726 78	$114,324 75.
and 25 other States & Territor's	64,667 22	167,379 48.

From which statement it appears that, notwithstanding Seamen arriving in the port of New York have paid $44,551 65 into the Fund, New York has received only $28,456 58 for taking care of them while sick; whereas California, Massachusetts, Louisiana, and Illinois, which have paid only $172 00 more, have received for the same purpose $114,324 75 in addition to large endowments for Marine Hospitals. If this representation be true, and it can be ascertained by referring to the Report in question, I presume a proper presentation of the facts to the next Congress, will lead to a large appropriation for a Marine Hospital at Quarantine.

I will conclude this paper with the following remarks of Mr. McCulloch.

"There is not on the Thames a lazaretto, where a ship from a suspected place may discharge her cargo and refit, so that it is detained, frequently at an enormous expense, during the whole period of Quarantine, while if she had perishable goods on board they may be very materially injured. The complaints of Quarantine grievances and oppressions are almost wholly occasioned by the want of proper facilities for its performance. Were these afforded, the burdens it imposes would be comparatively light, and we do not know that many more important services could be rendered to the country, than by constructing a proper Quarantine establishment."